THE
CLIMB

SUSANNAII BRIN

Artesian **Press**

P.O. Box 355, Buena Park, CA 90621

Take Ten Books
Thrillers

Bronco Buster	1-58659-041-3
Audio Cassette	1-58659-046-4
Audio CD	1-58659-325-0
The Climb	**1-58659-042-1**
Audio Cassette	**1-58659-047-2**
Audio CD	**1-58659-326-9**
Search and Rescue	1-58659-043-X
Audio Cassette	1-58659-048-0
Audio CD	1-58659-327-7
Timber	1-58659-044-8
Audio Cassette	1-58659-049-9
Audio CD	1-58659-328-5
Tough Guy	1-58659-045-6
Audio Cassette	1-58659-050-2
Audio CD	1-58659-329-3

Other Take Ten Themes:

Mystery	**Sports**	**Adventure**
Chillers	**Fantasy**	**Horror**
Disaster	**Romance**	

Development & Production: Laurel Associates, Inc.
Editor: Molly Mraz
Cover Illustrator: Fujiko
Graphic Design: Tony Amaro
©2004 Artesian Press

www.artesianpress.com

ISBN 1-58659-042-1

CONTENTS

Chapter 1

As the fishing boat neared the rocky beach of Thomas Bay, Badger Hintoc grabbed his backpack and his skis. "Get your gear!" he said to John Martini, who was staring up at the ice field. As the boat rocked in the shallow water, Badger leapt ashore, being careful to keep his shoes dry. The last thing he needed on the week-long climb was wet feet.

John Martini landed on the beach next to Badger. Grinning, he shifted his backpack. "I can't believe I'm finally here," he said, staring at the glacier fields. Then he looked toward the mountains that formed the boundary between Alaska and Canada. "Ever since I started climbing, I've dreamed of coming to Alaska and climbing the Devil's Thumb."

Badger frowned. "I told you, we're not climbing up that peak. It's too dangerous. We're going to climb one of the unnamed boundary peaks." He squinted at the early June sky and saw that it was clear. He prayed that the weather would hold through the week. He knew how quickly it could change.

Anger flared in John's eyes as he looked at Badger. He was used to getting his own way. After all, he figured, he was paying for Badger's services as a guide. "Look, I told you I've climbed just about everything in California, Arizona, and Oregon. I'm not a beginner."

"Yeah, I know you said you climbed Mt. Hood and El Capitan in Yosemite— but this is *Alaska.* Conditions are different here. You'll see. We'd better get going if we want to set up camp before dark," said Badger firmly.

John nodded, not pushing it. The last thing he wanted was for Badger to quit before they even started. There was time enough to get him to change his mind once they'd crossed the glaciers to the base of the mountain range.

After helping each other secure their backpacks, they headed for the glacier, which was visible in the distance. They walked a mile across the gravelly beach, their full packs heavy on their backs. Reaching the point where the glacier met the beach, Badger stopped and fitted his steel-spiked crampons to his hiking boots.

"I thought we were going to *ski* from here to the valley," said John, thinking it would be faster that way. His pack felt like it weighed a ton.

Badger shook his head and pointed at the ice. "Do you see any snow on that ice?" he asked rather sarcastically.

John stared at the end of the glacier. The ice was studded with small black rocks. He reached for his crampons without another word.

Scrambling up onto the lip of the glacier, Badger reached down and helped John up, giving him a reassuring smile. "We should reach snow about five miles up the valley."

"Good. I'm not used to being a pack horse," grumbled John, shifting the thirty-some-pound weight on his back.

Badger laughed. "You stateside guys have it too easy. I bet you drive right up to the base of a mountain, strap on all your climbing gear, and climb."

"It's not quite *that* simple," John shot back. Then he lightened up, thinking it was silly of him to be so uptight. "I guess I thought you guys up here have snowmobiles or dog sleds."

"We do, but they don't climb four-thousand-foot mountains," grinned Badger as they headed up the glacier. The gravel and ice under the weight of their steel-spiked crampons made a crunching sound as they walked.

They hiked in silence for several miles, grunting under the weight of their backpacks. John walked next to Badger, glad that he wasn't alone. There was something menacing about the miles of ice and the deadly quiet of the place. It was spooky somehow. "You been climbing long?" asked John. He only knew that Badger was nineteen years old, like himself, and had a reputation for being one of the best climbing guides in Alaska.

"Ever since I could walk," answered Badger. "How about you?"

"My parents had this thing about nature walks. But I got bored with walking, so I started climbing whatever was alongside the path. I progressed to rock climbing, then to mountains. Mom says I'm a 'height freak.' She doesn't like me climbing."

"Yeah, same with my mom. She thinks it's dangerous," agreed Badger.

"But that's what I like best," said John. He thought about the rush that filled him whenever he conquered a mountain and stood on its summit.

Badger shot John an uneasy look. There was a lot of danger where they were going. He hoped John didn't get his kicks from being reckless. "You'll get your fill of danger out here."

"Don't get me wrong, I'm not a fool. I *am* a careful climber. There's just something about overcoming all the obstacles of the mountain—beating the odds—that makes me feel alive," explained John, sensing Badger's worry.

"Good. I don't want to lose my life because you need a high," snapped Badger, thinking of all the dangers that could lie ahead.

John's anger flared. "Look, man. I'm an experienced climber. And yeah, I *like* to take risks—which is more than I can say for you. You're the one who won't climb Devil's Thumb."

Badger stopped and took a deep breath. Then he straightened to his full height of five feet, ten inches. "That's right, I won't. So if you think that we're going to get up to the base of the mountains, and then you're going to talk me into it, forget it!"

John held up his hands in a gesture of peace. The last thing he wanted to do was turn back. "Okay, okay, you're the guide. We'll climb this unnamed peak you've picked."

They continued on in silence, each wrapped in his own thoughts. When they finally reached the snowline, they had covered five miles. Badger slipped off his pack and rested for a moment before taking off his crampons.

"Boy, am I glad to see this snow. The going will be easier and faster on skis," said John, acting as if there'd been no harsh words between them.

"And more dangerous. The snow hides the cracks—the crevasses—in the glacier," explained Badger as he took a long rope from his pack. He clipped the rope to the harness that circled his waist and threw the rest to John.

"How deep are these crevasses?" asked John, staring out at the vast snow field. To him the scene looked as peaceful and safe as a baby's soft blanket dropped upon the ice.

"Hundreds of feet deep," answered Badger. He smiled to himself as John reached for the rope.

Chapter 2

"It's incredible!" exclaimed John, feeling suddenly afraid. The icefall before them was crisscrossed with wide crevasses that were as wide as forty feet across. In some of the crevasses were huge, unstable-looking blocks of ice that had broken off the glacier as it had melted and moved. "Are we going to cross that icefall?"

"Sure. We need to get to the top of the glacier plateau. That's where we'll set up base camp," answered Badger, scanning the sky. Puffy white snow clouds were beginning to form.

"Are you *sure* there's no other way?" asked John.

Badger gave him a sharp look. "Do you want to turn back?"

John laughed to hide his fear. "No! I was just surprised to see so many deep crevasses."

"Just keep a safe distance behind me. If we run into trouble, we've got each other," instructed Badger. Then he sized up the area and chose a route.

For the rest of the afternoon, they climbed up the icefall. As they climbed, they could hear the ice cracking and groaning. The constant noise coming from the glacier began to set John's nerves on edge.

"I never knew that a glacier made noise!" he yelled to Badger.

Badger called back, "It's straining to move! Don't worry about it."

"Easy for *you* to say," mumbled John to himself. He imagined the ice splitting open and himself falling into a hole so deep that no one would ever find him. Caught up in his thoughts, he veered to the right, creating a new set of footprints in the snow. Distracted by worry, he veered to the right of Badger's footprints.

Badger felt the rope tighten on his waist. Wondering why John had changed course, he glanced back. As he started to yell out, a snow bridge gave way under John's foot.

John snatched back his foot from the hole that had opened up. He looked down, but the hole was so deep he couldn't see the bottom. Frozen to the spot, he started to shake.

Badger worked his way back to John and called to him. "Careful, now! Move to your left." John did as he was told without taking his eyes off his feet. "See my footprints? Step where *I* stepped." Badger carefully kept his voice calm so as not to frighten John into moving too quickly.

When John reached Badger, he sank to his knees and vomited in the snow. He'd never had such a close call before!

Badger waited in silence. He knew

what it was like to brush up against death, to feel its icy fingers pulling at you. When John was finally calmed down, Badger gave him a hand up.

"Thanks a lot," John said stiffly. Embarrassed, he avoided Badger's eyes.

"You have to pay attention up here. You can't lose your concentration for one minute," warned Badger. Then he turned and continued up the icefall.

After another hour, they reached the plateau of the glacier. By now the sun was starting to go down, and a wind had come up. Overhead, the sky was a gray mass of clouds.

Badger saw that John looked ready to drop. "We can set up base camp here or move farther up the plateau," he said, giving John the choice.

John didn't want to walk another step. He was tired and cold to the bone. "Let's go up farther. I don't want to listen to the ice groaning all night," he said, not wanting Badger to know how terribly cold and tired he really was.

They continued on until dark. As they finally set up their tent, the wind whipped at their clothes, and snow began to fall.

"Just in time," said Badger as he zipped the flap of the tent closed.

"Yeah," answered John, rolling out his sleeping bag. "But it's not much warmer in here. Why, it must be below zero outside."

Badger laughed. "It probably is." He handed John a bag of trail mix and some dried fish.

"Remind me to bring a chef on my next expedition," joked John, eagerly reaching out for the food.

"I don't want to risk setting up the cookstove inside the tent," answered Badger. "But if you want to, you can go outside and fire it up. Maybe make yourself some hot cereal."

"No way. I'm half-frozen as it is," yawned John. "And exhausted." He slipped into his sleeping bag. Just minutes later, he was sound asleep.

Badger shook his head. *Today was nothing*, he thought to himself. The real challenge still lay ahead.

Chapter 3

Badger rose early to check the weather. The snow had stopped. The sky was clear. *Perfect day for climbing,* he thought as he went back into the tent to wake John. "Rise and shine!"

"Go away," mumbled John, pulling his bag around his ears.

"Get up, John. It's a good day for climbing. Up here in Alaska we have to take advantage of good weather. I'll get breakfast going while you dress." Then Badger picked up the cookstove and carried it outside.

Minutes later, as the oatmeal was coming to a boil, John stepped out of the tent. He stretched and looked around in amazement. "Boy, it sure did snow a lot last night!"

"Yeah. I'm afraid the going will be rough this morning," answered Badger. He dished up the cereal and handed John a bowl.

As John ate, he stared south toward a huge mountain peak. "That's Kate's Needle, isn't it?"

"Yes. It's on the Canadian side. And look—just to the north of us is the Devil's Thumb."

"It sure doesn't look that far to Kate's Needle," said John, hoping that Badger would reconsider.

Badger frowned. He knew what John was getting at. "Look, I'm *not* taking you up Kate's Needle. We don't have the supplies, and it's farther away than you think. It would mean another whole day of crisscrossing crevasses. And I don't think you really like crevasses that much."

Remembering how he'd put his foot through a snow bridge and almost fallen to his death, John backed off.

"You're right. I guess this unnamed peak of yours will be difficult enough."

Badger laughed. "It's no stroll in the park. I think you'll get your money's worth of difficulty." He pointed toward the unnamed peak that rose some four thousand feet into the air.

They stowed their skis and extra gear in the tent. After strapping on their spiked crampons, they set off toward the rocky part of the mountain. To reach the rocky ledges, they had to cross another ice field covered with deep snow and crisscrossed with more crevasses. In each hand, Badger and John carried an ice axe.

Two and a half hours after they left base camp, John called out to Badger, telling him to stop.

"What's wrong?" Badger called back. He traced his steps back to John.

John was madly gulping in air. His chest heaved like a long-distance runner's as he tried to catch his breath.

Drops of sweat beaded his forehead.

"Are you okay?" asked Badger, reaching for his water bottle.

John waved the bottle away. "I just need a rest. We've been going nonstop for hours."

"We're almost to the rocky part of the mountain," explained Badger. He wondered why, if John was such a good climber, he seemed so out of shape. "Another half hour at the most."

"Good. Slogging through this deep snow is tiring me out," said John honestly. "I'm up to it—don't get me wrong. I just need a little break."

"No problem. We can take five minutes," teased Badger. He reached in his pack, pulled out a protein bar, and handed it to John. "Here."

"Thanks."

As John ate his protein bar, Badger studied him for any signs of extreme exhaustion and altitude sickness. Finally, he decided that John was fine—

a little out of condition, but fine.

"Okay, I'm ready," said John, giving Badger a smile.

"I'd guess we've got about an hour to go to reach that overhanging wall," Badger said. He pointed at a ledge that jutted out from the mountain.

"Okay, let's go for it." John picked up his ice pick and waited for Badger to lead the way.

Reaching the rock ledge, Badger and John climbed up the overhanging wall with the front points of their crampons. Then, together, they stared up at the vertical rock of mountain. Both young men knew that this was where the *real* climb would begin.

"Whoa, this is really steep!" said John, surprised.

"Not as steep as Kate's Needle!" answered Badger, studying the vertical rock for a way up. "I hadn't counted on that rime."

"What?" asked John.

"*Rime.* It's a crumbly coating of ice. It's too thin to put an ice axe into and get a good hold. What we need is some frozen melt water," explained Badger.

John eyed the slippery vertical. He couldn't see any place where they could get a good toehold.

"There!" said Badger, finally. He pointed to a snake of melt water that had frozen into a thin strip of ice. The strip twisted up the vertical some two hundred feet. "We'll go that way—and pray that the ice is thick enough to hold our weight."

Chapter 4

Using their crampons and ice axes, Badger and John slowly inched their way up the vertical of the mountain. In the beginning, Badger worried about John. He could feel him jerking on the rope that was tied between them. From years of climbing with a partner, he knew that John hadn't found a rhythm yet. His movements were clumsy and awkward—like he was unsure of himself and afraid of falling.

"Don't keep looking back over your shoulder!" Badger yelled. "Looking back only makes you think of falling. Concentrate. You have to trust your hands and feet, man."

"I'm trying!" John shouted back, surprised that Badger could feel his fear. Then he got angry. *He probably thinks I'm a real wimp*, he thought to himself. Then, using his anger as fuel, he concentrated on finding a rhythm.

Minutes later, Badger smiled to himself. The jerky movements of the rope had become steadier. John had found a rhythm. Badger didn't think less of John for being afraid. He guessed most climbers were afraid at some point on the mountain. *He* was. It was a matter of accepting the danger— and then going beyond it to self-trust.

For the last five hundred feet, Badger and John climbed in unison. They swung their ice axes into the frozen melt water and kicked their toe points into the ice. Up, up, up they went, like the hands of a clock slowly moving toward twelve.

Swing, kick, swing, kick, thought Badger, losing himself in the rhythm. Suddenly he heard a *twang*. He froze against the mountain wall and struck out with his axe again. Again he heard the gut-wrenching *twang*. He knew what *that* sound meant. It meant that he'd hit solid rock.

Badger motioned for John to stop climbing. Then he swung his ice axe in an arc, looking for a place where the axes could grab a good hold. But everywhere he looked, he saw a thin layer of frost on the rock wall. "We've got to go back down," he yelled.

"*Come on*, Badger! We're almost to the overhanging ledge!" shouted John, not wanting to turn around.

"The melt water up here is too thin to support our weight. It's only frost. Stay there. I'll climb back to you." Slowly, Badger retraced his steps.

"Are you *sure* the ice is too thin?" asked John, giving Badger a hard, suspicious look.

"I told you—it's just frost up there over solid rock," answered Badger. Together, they looked back down the mountain. They were more than a thousand feet in the air, hanging from the mountainside. Badger felt his heart pumping hard with fear. He knew John was afraid, too. "Let's go down a hundred feet. From there we can look for another way up," suggested Badger as he carefully moved around John.

John nodded, too scared to answer. He'd never been in a situation like this before. He didn't know what else to do except to follow Badger's lead.

Together, they descended to a small outcropping of rocks. To settle his nerves, Badger took a deep breath. "Sorry. I thought the frozen ribbon of melt water went all the way up to the overhang."

"It's not your fault. From here it sure looks like it does," said John. He was glad to be on solid ground. His whole body shook with relief.

Badger glanced up and saw that clouds were beginning to form. He hoped it wouldn't snow again. "Maybe we should head back to camp. Clouds are shaping up like yesterday. Could mean another bad night."

"No! We're already behind schedule. If we go back to camp now, we won't ever reach the summit," John groaned. He couldn't stand to think that the mountain had defeated them.

"Why take a chance? We've only got food for today. Weather up here in Alaska isn't like it is down stateside. Up here it can be nice one minute and a raging blizzard the next," explained Badger. He reached in his pocket and pulled out a protein bar.

But John wasn't listening. He was studying the vertical of the mountain. "Look—over there at the southern edge of the mountain. There's a way up. See that frozen snake of ice?"

Badger nodded. He did see it. It looked thick. He wondered why he'd missed it earlier. It looked like a better route than the one they'd taken.

"We should have taken that way this morning," John grumbled. He thought that maybe Badger didn't know so much after all. "I say we climb that." He looked at his watch and saw that it was one o'clock. "We've got plenty of time."

Badger hesitated. He didn't like the idea of starting out again—especially with the way the sky looked.

"It didn't snow until after dark last night. We've got plenty of time to reach the summit and get back," snapped John, losing patience.

"Yes, but—"

"I hired you to get me to the summit. And we'd be there by now if you hadn't picked the wrong way up," said John. He stared hard at Badger, challenging him to live up to his reputation.

Badger thought for a minute. It was true that his earlier decision had been a mistake. *Maybe* they could make it up and back before nightfall. Then, against his better judgment, he agreed.

Chapter 5

Badger and John lost no time in getting to the southern side of the mountain. There, Badger studied the snake of ice that twisted its way up. The ice looked plenty thick and solid. "I don't think we'll have any trouble climbing here," he said. But for a moment he didn't move, noticing that the clouds had thickened and a slight breeze had come up.

"Let's go for it, man!" barked John, excited by the thought that they could make it to the summit after all.

"I don't know, John. The weather is changing." Badger tried to weigh the possibilities. He figured they could probably make it to the summit. But there was a slim possibility that they could get trapped on the mountain in a snowstorm.

"Look, I've paid you to guide me. If you don't *want* to, I'll just climb by myself," growled John. He wasn't going to let Badger stop him now. Not when he was so close to reaching his goal. After all, he'd been wanting to climb a peak in Alaska for years.

"Part of my job as a guide is make sure that I get you back to town *alive*," snapped Badger, losing his patience. He was tired of John's attitude.

John readjusted the crampons on his shoes. Then he stood up and glared at Badger. "Don't worry about it—you're fired. I can get myself back to town alive without you."

Badger was stunned. He'd never been fired before. Then he was angry—angrier than he'd ever been in his life. "You think you're so tough. Well, go ahead! Climb the mountain alone, wise guy. But if you get in trouble up there, don't bother calling out for help. No one will be there to hear you."

John turned back to Badger and glared at him coldly. A minute went by. "Well, what are you hanging around for? I said that you're fired."

"*Fine!*" Badger was so angry he couldn't think. He turned and started back toward camp.

John began to climb the snake of ice that led up the mountain. At first the climb was easy, even fun. He smiled to himself. He didn't need a guide. Why, he'd climbed *hundreds* of rocks and mountains in the lower states.

Badger was so upset that he didn't look back as he hiked across the rocky part of the mountain bordering the ice field. *I don't need this,* he thought. *Rich guys like John are a pain. They come up here to Alaska and act like they know it all. They don't know anything!*

It took Badger an hour to reach the spot where they'd climbed up the ice field. Stopping to take his ice axes from his pack, he studied the snow-covered field. Some of the snow had melted. Several crevasses were clearly visible. *It'll be easier going down than it was coming up*, he thought, remembering how John had almost fallen through a snow bridge into a crevasse.

Badger looked back at the mountain. He could see John climbing. John was halfway up the vertical. He would surely make it to the summit if the weather held. But overhead, the clouds were steadily growing darker.

Moving across the snow-covered ice field, Badger forgot about John and the weather. He concentrated on the downhill climb, carefully avoiding a fall into a crevasse. The going was faster now that some of the snow had melted. In a few places he could see the tracks that they'd made earlier.

It took Badger only two hours to get to their base camp. He took off his pack and dropped it inside the tent. Then he went back outside and saw that large snowflakes had already begun to fall. The earlier breeze had grown stronger. Now it was a cold wind.

Badger looked at the falling snow and cursed. He'd had a hunch it would snow again. He realized that he should have *made* John listen. Now he was alone on the mountain in a snowstorm.

Looking up, he tried to locate John on the mountain—but he couldn't see him. Too much snow was falling.

I shouldn't have let him go on alone, thought Badger, berating himself for letting a moment's anger cloud his judgment. Ducking back into the tent, he packed their lightweight sleeping bags into tight rolls. Then he quickly made several sandwiches.

Badger ate one of the sandwiches as he stuffed trail mix and the rest of the sandwiches into his pack. Then, pulling on his ski mask and a pair of snow goggles, he went back outside. It was snowing harder now.

Badger was tired and upset with himself. He'd acted unprofessionally—and he knew it. Now he had to make it right. With a weary sigh, he headed back up the mountain. He prayed that he would be able to find John before it was too late.

Chapter 6

The snow was falling in thick sheets when Badger started across the ice field. The wind blew the giant flakes straight at him. He couldn't see more than two feet in front of him. Every few feet, he had to stop and wipe the snow from his goggles.

Using his ice axes like a blind man uses a cane, Badger felt the ground in front of him before he took a step forward. He didn't want to fall into a crevasse. Thoughts of death swirled through his mind. He knew it was his fault that John was up on the mountain alone. He should have forced him to return to camp. So what if they had come to blows? *I should never have let that stubborn fool get under my skin that way*, Badger thought. *I let my anger get the best of me, and now our lives are at stake.*

Stopping to get his bearings, Badger straightened and looked around. He couldn't see the mountain. He looked up at the night sky and couldn't see that, either. The cloud cover was so low and the snowfall so thick that everything was white. "This is just g   r   e   a   t   — a *whiteout*," he grumbled out loud. He prayed that John had found a ledge or an outcropping of rocks—some place where he could take shelter from the dangerous weather.

Badger forced himself to pick up the pace. The image of John freezing to death up on the mountain urged him on. It was tough going against the wind-driven snow. The added weight of his pack didn't help, either.

Twice, one of his ice axes crashed through a layer of snow into the yawning emptiness of a crevasse. Both times he had to stop for a moment to shake off his fear. And both times he had to reach deep inside himself for the courage to go on. He knew that no sensible climber would try crossing an ice field in such weather. But he had no choice. He *had* to get to John.

Four hours later Badger reached the rocky part of the mountain. It had taken him twice the usual time. He wanted to sit down and rest, but he couldn't. He had to keep going. Tired and shivering from the cold wind, he continued southward—toward the place where he'd last seen John.

The snow was falling heavily when Badger reached the snake of ice that twisted up the vertical of the unnamed peak. He hesitated. *Climbing in this whiteout is crazy*, he told himself. Doubts began to fill his mind. *I'll be like a blind man crawling along the edge of a canyon.* He hugged himself, trying to get warm.

But it didn't help.

Finally, he began the ascent.

Trust your hands and feet, he told himself. *Trust. And concentrate.* Over and over again, his ice axe dug into the snake of ice as he steadily worked his way upward. Every so often he stopped and called out, "John! John!" But his voice was carried away on the wind. He had no way of knowing if John heard him. He kept climbing, climbing, inching his way upward.

Exhausted, but still fueled with determination, Badger emptied his mind of everything except climbing. When he was up about a thousand feet, he stopped. The snowfall had lightened. Now he could see better. A few feet above his head and to the right, he saw a slim ledge of rocks. He called out, "John! Are you up there? John!"

For a moment, he heard nothing but the howling of the wind. Then he heard a faint voice calling his name.

"Badger, is that you?" John called weakly. Slowly, he moved to the rocky edge and looked down.

"Hold tight! I'm coming up," Badger called out. He'd never been so happy to see anyone in his life. Moving slowly, he carefully inched his way up and over the ledge.

"I can't believe it's you!" cried John. His voice trembled with relief and tears of happiness.

"Well, I couldn't leave you to freeze to death—even if you *did* fire me," joked Badger, hiding his concern. John was shivering so hard he looked like a dog shaking water from his coat. Ice had formed on his blond eyebrows and at the edges of his knit cap. Quickly, Badger untied one of the sleeping bags from his pack and wrapped it around the shivering young man.

"All the comforts of home," croaked John. The skin on his lips began to crack and bleed as he tried to smile.

"Yeah, look! I even brought you a gourmet meal." Badger dug in his pack and pulled out two sandwiches and a chocolate bar.

John gulped down the food. Between bites, he tried to thank Badger for coming back. "You were right, man. I shouldn't have started to climb."

"Yeah, and I shouldn't have *let* you," Badger shot back. "So forget it. Besides, this will be quite an adventure. I've never slept on a ledge during a whiteout before—not a thousand feet up, anyway!"

"It's not pleasant, let me tell you," John laughed weakly, pulling the warm sleeping bag closer. Then his blue eyes turned serious. "I've been fighting sleep for the last few hours. I was afraid I wouldn't wake up."

"You'll be okay in that bag. It's made for forty-below weather." Badger unrolled his own sleeping bag and climbed into it.

"Thanks, man. You saved my life," John said, his voice full of emotion.

"It's what you paid me the big bucks for," joked Badger, glad that he'd made it. He didn't tell John about the two times he'd almost fallen into a crevasse or what a struggle it had been to get to him.

"Well, I was sure being a jerk," said John. "I guess I thought I knew everything. Anyway—I'm sorry."

"Forget it." Badger yawned. He was exhausted. Every inch of his body ached. "Get some sleep now. You'll need it for tomorrow."

The snow started falling again, thick and fast. John was about to pull the bag over his head when a new worry hit him. "How long do you figure it's going to snow?"

"You'd better hope that it stops tonight—for both our sakes," mumbled Badger. Right now he was too tired to think about what lay ahead.

Chapter 7

When Badger woke up, he found himself completely covered with snow. Shaking off the thick white blanket, he eased himself up into a sitting position. Glancing over at John's bag, he saw that it was covered with snow, too. Quickly, he brushed the heavy snow from the top of the bag. Then, slowly, John emerged.

"Hey! Is that a nice way to wake up a guy?" grinned John, taking off his cap and shaking it. "I had this dream that I was buried alive."

"There wasn't *that* much snow on you," laughed Badger, relieved that sometime during the night, the snow had stopped. He looked up at the sky. It was light blue and cloudless. "Looks like we got lucky this time. The blizzard seems to be over for now."

"Good. Then we can finish our climb. I figure it's only about two thousand feet to the summit." John rummaged in his backpack, looking for something to eat. The only thing he could find was a small box of raisins. He offered them to Badger, who shook his head *no.*

Badger stared at John in surprise. His brown eyes were dark as the rocks on the mountain. "Climb to the *summit?* I think we should head back to base camp. The weather pattern seems to be nice mornings followed by afternoon clouds, and then snow. I don't want to spend another night on this ledge."

"I don't either, but I think we can make it to the summit and back down before the weather changes," said John. He stared up at the mountain's peak with a sense of longing.

Badger wasn't sure. They could

make it if the climb went smoothly—
without any hitches at all. Still, the
safest thing to do was to return to base
camp. He glanced at John. He saw by
the fire in John's eyes that he meant to
climb. In his heart, Badger wanted to
reach the summit, too. Finally, he
shrugged and nodded. "Let's go for it."

"Well, *all right!*" John grinned. The
summit would be theirs after all!

"Here's half a sandwich," said
Badger, biting into the other half.

"Thanks." John ate his sandwich in
two bites. "It's beautiful up here." From
where they stood, John could see for
miles. Below them stretched the glacier
valley, white and glistening in the sun.
To the left and right rose the majestic
peaks of the boundary mountains.

Badger finished strapping on his
crampons. "I like the quiet, but we'd
better get going. We'll leave everything
here except our ice axes."

"Good idea," answered John,

knowing that they would be able to climb faster without the weight of their heavy packs and bags.

"We're going to have to push ourselves to get to the top and back before the weather changes," said Badger, starting to climb the rock face.

John followed. He was still cold, but after a few minutes of climbing, his body warmed. He had to scramble to keep up with Badger, who was climbing at a fast, steady pace. *He moves as lightly as a hummingbird*, John thought to himself as he sucked in deep breaths of crisp, cold air.

The mountain was crisscrossed with small snow fields, icy gaps, and small rocky steps. The tiny steps made the climbing almost easy. *This would be fun*, thought Badger, *if we didn't have to worry about the weather.*

John didn't know how long they'd been climbing when he saw Badger stop and look up. "What's wrong?"

John yelled. He knew that it couldn't be the sky. It was still clear.

"Nothing!" Badger shouted back. "Just looking for a quicker way up." All morning he'd zigzagged his way back and forth across the mountain. It was the easiest path. He knew they could continue the pattern to the top. Going straight up the face would be a much harder climb.

John caught up to Badger. He was breathing hard, and sweat was beading his forehead. "You thinking of going straight up?" he asked, following the direction of Badger's gaze.

"It will be a lot faster. I want to get off this mountain before the weather changes. Are you up to it?"

John swallowed hard. The face was very steep and patched with thin ice. Then he grinned and shouted, "Lead the way!"

Badger checked the ropes joining them, to be sure they were secure. "See you at the top!" he yelled. Then he started climbing straight up.

John followed, swinging his axe into the ice-covered rock. The ice was thin, and the climb steep. The steady thunk of Badger's ice axe biting into the ice reassured him. But a few minutes later, he heard the axe hit solid rock. He stopped and looked up.

Badger swung his pick to the right. He hit rock. Again and again he tried to find some ice that was thick enough to hold his weight.

John cringed every time he heard the dull clanking sound of the axe on rock. He knew that if Badger didn't find a hold, they'd have to go down and find another way up. Hanging from his ice axes, John glanced down. He felt his stomach rise into his throat. They were over two thousand feet in the air. The glacier field and base camp were far, far below them.

As Badger swung out and up one

more time, the ice axe felt heavy in his hand. Then he heard a *thunk* and felt the axe dig into ice. *Nice, thick ice,* he thought, pleased that they could continue. He quickly pulled himself up the next few feet of mountain.

Again, John followed. But his mind was tormented with visions of falling. He tried to concentrate, but he couldn't. Fear seemed to be riding him, erasing all he knew about climbing.

Badger could feel the rope that was connecting the two of them begin to jerk awkwardly. *Not again,* he thought to himself, knowing instantly that John had looked down the mountain. "Don't look down!" he yelled back over his shoulder.

John didn't answer. He'd stopped climbing and was staring down, as if in a trance. Fear had immobilized him, freezing his muscles. Yet he could hear Badger yelling at him.

"This time I'm not going to climb

back down to you, John! If you don't start climbing, I'll drag your sorry self all the way to the summit! " barked Badger. He meant it, too.

John didn't move.

He's going to get us both killed if he doesn't start climbing, thought Badger. Now he seriously began to doubt whether John had really climbed all those mountains stateside. Finally, he decided to start making chicken sounds. His hope was that his taunting would anger John into moving.

Sure enough, when John heard the chicken sounds, anger snaked through his body. The spell of sheer terror was broken. He swung out with his axe and started climbing again. "*Nobody* calls *me* a chicken!" he screamed at Badger. All he wanted was to catch up with Badger and punch him in the face.

Badger grinned. His plan had worked! He continued upward. An hour later, he reached a wide expanse of rock almost like a ledge. The summit was only a few feet above. Excitement and fear filled his chest as he swung his ice axe over the top. For a moment he prayed silently that the axe would hold—and it did. Quickly, he scrambled up the last few feet, using his crampons to climb the thinly iced rock.

Moments later, John joined him on the summit. They grinned at each other. John put out his gloved hand to Badger. "Give me five, man." They slapped hands and laughed.

Badger looked out at the majestic landscape of icy snow and rock. The beauty of the lonely mountain range never failed to fill him with awe.

"That is *some* view," murmured John, feeling a rush of emotion. "Being up here really makes me feel alive."

"Yeah, I know what you mean," Badger said. He stared at the sky. In the distance, he could see dark clouds sweeping in from the south.

Chapter 8

John didn't argue with Badger about leaving the summit. He wanted to go. The wind was blowing hard, making it difficult even to stand up. The standing space on top of the summit was no bigger than a kitchen table. John knew that a wrong step in any direction would send him to his death.

"I'm starting down, now," said Badger, hanging a small camera around his neck. "When I'm down a few feet, I'll lean out and take your picture. Then you can prove to your buddies that you really made it to the summit."

"Hey, *thanks*, Badger! I didn't think of bringing a camera along," said John, realizing that Badger was really trying to help him after all.

Badger climbed down to the shoulder of the mountain and took several pictures of John. Then he motioned for him to start his descent.

"Wow! It's sure a lot easier coming down," said John, joining Badger on the shoulder.

Badger frowned. "Don't get careless. I've seen more climbers hurt coming down the mountain than going up."

"Yeah, I know. But lighten up, will you, man? We did what we set out to do." John grinned, wincing with the pain of stretching his cracked lips.

"Well, my job isn't over yet. Not until I get you safely back to St. Petersburg," Badger insisted. "So pay attention." Turning, he started climbing down the mountain again. He didn't like pulling rank like that. But he didn't want John to get hurt either.

Badger set a quick pace as they descended the mountain. He didn't like the look of the big, dark clouds that were gathering overhead. Another snowstorm was coming. At the ledge where they'd spent the night, they retrieved their stuff and continued on.

Two hours later they dropped down from the rocky, vertical part of the mountain to the ice field. John stopped to rest. Taking off a glove, he wiped sweat from his forehead. He was breathing heavily, nearly panting. "I've *got* to take a rest, man. I'm beat."

"Not now. We have to keep going. It will take us another three hours to cross the ice field and get back to base camp," said Badger as he studied the afternoon sky, which was still darkening with clouds.

"Come on! Just for five or ten minutes?" whined John, starting to slide his pack off his back. His aching legs and back trembled with exhaustion.

Badger rushed over to stop him from taking off his pack. "I said *no!* I don't want to get caught on the ice field in a snowstorm. There's no protection out there. We have to get to base camp *now*."

"Go without me, then. I know how to get back." John was irritated. It seemed that Badger had been telling him what to do the whole trip. He was tired of being bossed around.

"I did that yesterday, remember?" Badger felt like shaking some sense into John, but he controlled his anger. "I'm tired, too. But I'll tie you up and drag you across that ice field if I have to."

John could tell by the expression on Badger's face that he was serious. Too tired to fight, he gave in. "All right! We'll do it your way."

With Badger leading the way, they started across the ice field. In some places the wind had blown the snow away, leaving the crevasses clearly visible. But Badger didn't take any chances. He used his ice axes like sticks, poking the ground, looking for snow bridges or a sheet of thin ice covering a dangerous crevasse.

John staggered along behind Badger. He was exhausted. He wanted to curl up into a ball and sleep. Twice he fell. Both times, Badger forced him to get up and continue.

Hours passed as they trudged slowly across the ice field. Badger figured they had only a short way to go when it started to snow. Once it started, the snow came down in sheets, just like it had the night before. Within minutes, Badger couldn't see more than a few feet in any direction. He stopped and waited for John to catch up.

John couldn't see. He tried to blink rapidly—anything to keep the snow from stinging his eyes. Yet no matter how he strained to see through the thickly falling snow, he couldn't. Everything was white. It was like he was trapped inside a cotton ball. Panic gripped his chest. He didn't know which way to turn. He yelled Badger's name.

"Follow the rope!" Badger yelled back. He gave a tug on the length of rope that tied them together.

"The rope, the rope," repeated John, trying to think clearly. But he couldn't see Badger's footsteps. The snow had covered them. He was afraid to walk forward, afraid he'd fall into a crevasse.

"Come on! Follow the rope!" Badger yelled again, yanking on the rope as hard as he could.

John staggered from the sharp tug of the rope. Then he snapped to his senses. Slowly, he walked forward, letting the rope reel him in.

Badger patted him on the back and smiled. "Only a little way more to go, John. Then you can curl up in the tent and go to sleep, all nice and warm."

Within a few minutes, they were back at base camp. Quickly, Badger unzipped the tent and followed John inside. John dropped his pack and slumped down on the floor of the tent. "I feel like I climbed the whole *range* of mountains out there today!" He smiled weakly at Badger.

"We covered a lot of ground," laughed Badger. He, too, was grateful to be back in the tent, safe from the storm. He'd done his job. Tomorrow they'd head for home.

John sat up and looked at Badger with respect. "I know I've been a pain this whole trip. Thanks for not leaving me. And for saving my life—twice. Now I know why you're called the best guide in Alaska."

"You'd have done the same for me," answered Badger, ducking his head shyly. Praise always made him feel uncomfortable and embarrassed.

John swallowed hard. He was so ashamed of how he'd acted. He wanted the two of them to be friends. "Look, if you come down to California, I'll show you all the sights. And we can climb any mountain you want."

Badger thought for a moment and then grinned. "How about we just go to a warm, sunny beach?"

Smiling, both young men snuggled into the warmth of their sleeping bags. Outside, the wind howled and the snow continued to fall.